Donated to
SAINT PAUL PUBLIC LIBRARY

THE SINGING GEESE

retold by Jan Wahl

illustrated by Sterling Brown

Dutton LODESTAR New York

LEXINGTON

for Liz and Ed Koster
J.W.
to my daughter, Briana Jewel Brown
S.B.

Text copyright © 1998 by Jan Wahl

Illustrations copyright © 1998 by Sterling Brown

Library of Congress Cataloging-in-Publication Data

Wahl, Jan.
The singing geese: retold by Jan Wahl;
illustrated by Sterling Brown—1st ed.
p. cm.
Summary: Sam Bombel shoots a goose and brings it home
for his wife to cook for dinner, but when it is set on the table,
the other geese come to reclaim it.
ISBN 0-525-67499-3 (alk. paper)
[1. Afro-Americans— Folklore. 2. Folklore—Maryland. 3. Tall tales.]
I. Brown, Sterling, 1963— ill. II. Title.
PZ8.1.W126Si 1998
398.2'089'960752
[E]—DC20 96-30796 CIP AC

Published in the United States by Lodestar Books,
an affiliate of Dutton Children's Books,
a member of Penguin Putnam Inc.,
375 Hudson Street, New York, New York 10014

Published simultaneously in Canada
by McClelland & Stewart, Toronto

Editor: Virginia Buckley   Designer: Dick Granald

Printed in Hong Kong   First Edition
10 9 8 7 6 5 4 3 2 1

Sam Bombel went out
one day to shoot his dinner.

He stopped right past the corn rows, and he stepped through a marsh until he heard a sound way above.

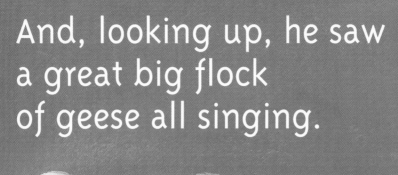

And, looking up, he saw
a great big flock
of geese all singing.

"La lee loo.
Come quilla, come quilla.
Bang, bang, bang!
Quilla bang."

Sam Bombel pointed his gun,
and he shot one of the geese.
And it sang all the way
down, down, down
as it fell.

"La lee loo.
Come quilla, come quilla.
Bang, bang, bang!
Quilla bang."

Sam Bombel took the goose home and told his wife, "Cook it for dinner."

And each feather, as she plucked it, flew out, out, out of the window.

She put the goose in the stove.
But all the time it was cooking
she heard strange
cackling sounds.

"La lee loo.
Come quilla, come quilla.
Bang, bang, bang!
Quilla bang."

When the goose was cooked,
she set it on the table.
But as Sam Bombel picked up knife and
fork to carve it, that goose called.

"La lee loo.
Come quilla, come quilla.
Bang, bang, bang!
Quilla bang."

When Sam Bombel was about to stick his knife in the goose, there came a *swooshing* yonder, and then a whole flock of geese flew through the window singing.

And each one stuck a feather back into that goose, and they lifted it up from the pot.

Then all and every one
flew out of the window singing.

"La lee loo.
Come quilla, come quilla.
Bang, bang, bang!
Quilla bang."

And Sam Bombel never went hunting again.

The Singing Geese

music by Elizabeth Koster

La   lee   loo.   Come quilla, come quilla.   Bang, bang, bang! Quil – la   bang.